Bierce, Ambrose
An Occurrence at Owl Creek Bridge

DATE DUE

The intervals of silence grew progressively longer,

the delays became maddening.

AN OCCURRENCE AT OWL CREEK BRIDGE

AMBROSE BIERCE

Creative Education

I

A man stood upon a railroad bridge in northern Alabama, looking down into the swift water twenty feet below. The man's hands were behind his back, the wrists bound with a cord. A rope closely encircled his neck. It was attached to a stout cross-timber above his head and the slack fell to the level of his knees. Some loose boards laid upon the sleepers supporting the metals of the railway supplied a footing for him and his executioners—two private soldiers of the Federal army, directed by a sergeant who in civil life may have been a deputy sheriff. At a short remove upon the same temporary platform was an officer in the uniform of his rank, armed. He was a captain. A sentinel at each end of the bridge stood with his rifle in the position known as "support," that is to say, vertical in front of the left shoulder, the hammer resting on the forearm thrown straight across the chest—a formal and unnatural position, enforcing an erect carriage of the body. It did not appear to be the duty of these two men to know what was occurring at the center of the bridge; they merely blockaded the two ends of the foot planking that traversed it.

Beyond one of the sentinels nobody was in sight; the railroad ran straight away into a forest for a hundred yards, then, curving, was lost to view. Doubtless there was an outpost farther along. The other bank of the stream was open ground—a gentle acclivity topped with a stockade of vertical tree trunks, loop-holed for rifles, with a single embrasure through which protruded the muzzle of a brass cannon commanding the bridge. Midway of the slope between the bridge and fort were the spectators—a single company of infantry in line, at "parade rest," the butts of the rifles on the ground, the barrels inclining slightly backward against the right shoulder, the hands crossed upon the stock. A lieutenant stood at the right of the line, the point of his sword upon the ground, his left hand resting upon his right. Excepting the group of four at the center of the bridge, not a man moved. The company faced the bridge, staring stonily, motionless. The sentinels, facing the banks of the stream, might have been statues to adorn the bridge. The captain stood with folded arms, silent, observing the work of his subordinates, but making no sign. Death is a dignitary who when he comes announced is to be received with formal manifestations of respect, even by those most familiar with him. In the code of military etiquette silence and fixity are forms of deference.

The man who was engaged in being hanged was apparently about thirty-five years of age. He was a civilian, if one might judge from his habit, which was that of a planter. His features were good—a straight nose,

A Civil War-era bridge

firm mouth, broad forehead, from which his long, dark hair was combed straight back, falling behind his ears to the collar of his well-fitting frock-coat. He wore a mustache and pointed beard, but no whiskers; his eyes were large and dark gray, and had a kindly expression which one would hardly have expected in one whose neck was in the hemp. Evidently this was no vulgar assassin. The liberal military code makes provision for hanging many kinds of persons, and gentlemen are not excluded.

The preparations being complete, the two private soldiers stepped aside and each drew away the plank upon which he had been standing. The sergeant turned to the captain, saluted and placed himself immediately behind that officer, who in turn moved apart one pace. These movements left the condemned man and the sergeant standing on the two ends of the same plank, which spanned three of the cross-ties of the bridge. The end upon which the civilian stood almost, but not quite, reached a fourth. This plank had been held in place by the weight of the captain; it was now held by that of the sergeant. At a signal from the former the latter would step aside, the plank would tilt and the condemned man go down between two ties. The arrangement commended itself to his judgment as simple and effective. His face had not been covered nor his eyes bandaged. He looked a moment at his "unsteadfast footing," then let his gaze wander to the swirling water of the stream racing madly beneath his feet. A piece of dancing driftwood caught his attention and his eyes followed it down the current. How slowly it appeared to move! What a sluggish stream!

He closed his eyes in order to fix his last thoughts upon his wife and children. The water, touched to gold by the early sun, the brooding mists under the banks at some distance down the stream, the fort, the soldiers, the piece of drift—all had distracted him. And now he became conscious of a new disturbance. Striking through the thought of his dear ones was a sound which he could neither ignore nor understand, a sharp, distinct, metallic percussion like the stroke of a blacksmith's hammer upon the anvil; it had the same ringing quality. He wondered what it was, and whether immeasurably distant or near by—it seemed both. Its recurrence was regular, but as slow as the tolling of a death knell. He awaited each stroke with impatience and—he knew not why—apprehension. The intervals of silence grew progressively longer, the delays became maddening. With their greater infrequency the sounds increased in strength and sharpness. They hurt his ear like the thrust of a knife; he feared he would shriek. What he heard was the ticking of his watch.

He unclosed his eyes and saw again the water below him. "If I could free my hands," he thought, "I might throw off the noose and spring into the stream. By diving I could evade the bullets and, swimming vigorously, reach the bank, take to the woods and get away home. My home, thank God, is as yet outside their lines; my wife and little ones are still beyond the invader's farthest advance."

As these thoughts, which have here to be set down in words, were flashed into the doomed man's brain rather than evolved from it the captain nodded to the sergeant. The sergeant stepped aside.

II

Peyton Farquhar was a well-to-do planter, of an old and highly respected Alabama family. Being a slave owner and like other slave owners a politician he was naturally an original secessionist and ardently devoted to the Southern cause. Circumstances of an imperious nature, which it is unnecessary to relate here, had prevented him from taking service with the gallant army that had fought the disastrous campaigns ending with the fall of Corinth, and he chafed under the inglorious restraint, longing for the release of his energies, the larger life of the soldier, the opportunity for distinction. That opportunity, he felt, would come, as it comes to all in war time. Meanwhile he did what he could. No service was too humble for him to perform in aid of the South, no adventure too perilous for him to undertake if consistent with the character of a civilian who was at heart a soldier, and who in good faith and without too much qualification assented to at least a part of the frankly villainous dictum that all is fair in love and war.

One evening while Farquhar and his wife were sitting on a rustic bench near the entrance to his grounds, a gray-clad soldier rode up to the gate and asked for a drink of water. Mrs. Farquhar was only too happy to serve him with her own white hands. While she was fetching the water her husband approached the dusty horseman and inquired eagerly for news from the front.

"The Yanks are repairing the railroads," said the man, "and are getting ready for another advance. They have reached the Owl Creek bridge, put it in order and built a stockade on the north bank. The commandant has issued an order, which is posted everywhere, declaring that any civilian caught interfering with the railroad, its bridges, tunnels or trains will be summarily hanged. I saw the order."

"How far is it to the Owl Creek bridge?" Farquhar asked.

"About thirty miles."

"Is there no force on this side of the creek?"

"Only a picket post half a mile out, on the railroad, and a single sentinel at this end of the bridge."

"Suppose a man—a civilian and student of hanging—should elude the picket post and perhaps get the better of the sentinel," said Farquhar, smiling, "what could he accomplish?"

The soldier reflected. "I was there a month ago," he replied. "I observed that the flood of last winter had lodged a great quantity of drift-wood against the wooden pier at this end of the bridge. It is now dry and would burn like tow."

The lady had now brought the water, which the soldier drank. He thanked her ceremoniously, bowed to her husband and rode away. An hour later, after nightfall, he repassed the plantation, going northward in the direction from which he had come. He was a Federal scout.

III

As Peyton Farquhar fell straight downward through the bridge he lost consciousness and was as one already dead. From this state he was awak-ened—ages later, it seemed to him—by the pain of a sharp pressure upon his throat, followed by a sense of suffocation. Keen, poignant agonies seemed to shoot from his neck downward through every fiber of his body and limbs. These pains appeared to flash along well-defined lines of ramification and to beat with an inconceivably rapid periodicity. They seemed like streams of pulsating fire heating him to an intolerable temperature. As to his head, he was conscious of nothing but a feeling of fullness—of congestion. These sensations were unaccompanied by thought. The intellectual part of his nature was already effaced; he had power only to feel, and feeling was torment. He was conscious of motion. Encompassed in a luminous cloud, of which he was now merely the fiery heart, without material substance, he swung through unthinkable arcs of oscillation, like a vast pendulum. Then all at once, with terrible suddenness, the light about him shot upward with the noise of a loud plash; a frightful roaring was in his ears, and all was cold and dark. The power of thought was restored; he knew that the rope had broken and he had fallen into the stream. There was no additional strangulation; the noose about his neck was already suffocating him and kept the water from his lungs. To die of hanging at the bottom of a river!—the idea seemed to him ludicrous. He opened his eyes in the darkness and saw above him a gleam of light, but how distant, how inaccessible! He was still sinking, for the light became fainter and fainter until it was a mere glimmer. Then it began to grow and brighten, and he knew that he was rising toward the surface—knew it with reluctance, for he was now very comfortable. "To be hanged and drowned," he thought, "that is not so bad; but I do not wish to be shot. No; I will not be shot; that is not fair."

He was not conscious of an effort, but a sharp pain in his wrist apprised him that he was trying to free his hands. He gave the struggle his attention, as an idler might observe the feat of a juggler, without interest in the outcome. What splendid effort!—what magnificent, what superhuman strength! Ah, that was a fine endeavor! Bravo! The cord fell away; his arms parted and floated upward, the hands dimly seen on each side in the growing light. He watched them with a new interest as first one and then the other pounced upon the noose at his neck. They tore it away and thrust it fiercely aside, its undulations resembling those of a water snake. "Put it back, put it back!" He thought he shouted these words to his hands, for the undoing of the noose had been succeeded by the direst pang that he had yet experienced. His neck ached horribly; his brain was on fire; his heart, which had been fluttering faintly, gave a great leap, trying to force itself out at his mouth. His whole body was racked and wrenched with an insupportable anguish! But his disobedient hands gave no heed to the command. They beat the water vigorously with quick, downward strokes, forcing him to the surface. He felt his head emerge;

his eyes were blinded by the sunlight; his chest expanded convulsively, and with a supreme and crowning agony his lungs engulfed a great draught of air, which instantly he expelled in a shriek!

He was now in full possession of his physical senses. They were, indeed, preternaturally keen and alert. Something in the awful disturbance of his organic system had so exalted and refined them that they made record of things never before perceived. He felt the ripples upon his face and heard their separate sounds as they struck. He looked at the forest on the bank of the stream, saw the individual trees, the leaves and the veining of each leaf—saw the very insects upon them: the locusts, the brilliant-bodied flies, the gray spiders stretching their webs from twig to twig. He noted the prismatic colors in all the dewdrops upon a million blades of grass. The humming of the gnats that danced above the eddies of the stream, the beating of the dragon-flies' wings, the strokes of the water-spiders' legs, like oars which had lifted their boat—all these made audible music. A fish slid along beneath his eyes and he heard the rush of its body parting the water.

He had come to the surface facing down the stream; in a moment the visible world seemed to wheel slowly round, himself the pivotal point, and he saw the bridge, the fort, the soldiers upon the bridge, the captain, the sergeant, the two privates, his executioners. They were in silhouette against the blue sky. They shouted and gesticulated, pointing at him. The captain had drawn his pistol, but did not fire; the others were unarmed. Their movements were grotesque and horrible, their forms gigantic.

Suddenly he heard a sharp report and something struck the water smartly within a few inches of his head, spattering his face with spray. He heard a second report, and saw one of the sentinels with his rifle at his shoulder, a light cloud of blue smoke rising from the muzzle. The man in the water saw the eye of the man on the bridge gazing into his own through the sights of the rifle. He observed that it was a gray eye and remembered having read that gray eyes were keenest, and that all famous marksmen had them. Nevertheless, this one had missed.

A counter-swirl had caught Farquhar and turned him half round; he was again looking into the forest on the bank opposite the fort. The sound of a clear, high voice in a monotonous singsong now rang out behind him and came across the water with a distinctness that pierced and subdued all other sounds, even the beating of the ripples in his ears. Although no soldier, he had frequented camps enough to know the dread significance of that deliberate, drawling, aspirated chant; the lieutenant on shore was taking a part in the morning's work. How coldly and pitilessly—with what an even, calm intonation, presaging, and enforcing tranquility in the men—with what accurately measured intervals fell those cruel words:

"Attention, company! . . . Shoulder arms! . . . Ready! . . . Aim! . . . Fire!"

Farquhar dived—dived as deeply as he could. The water roared in his ears like the voice of Niagara, yet he heard the dulled thunder of the volley and, rising again toward the surface, met shining bits of metal, singularly flattened, oscillating slowly downward. Some of them touched him on the face and hands, then fell away, continuing their descent. One lodged between his collar and neck; it was uncomfortably warm and he snatched it out.

As he rose to the surface, gasping for breath, he saw that he had been a long time under water; he was perceptibly farther down stream—nearer to safety. The soldiers had almost finished reloading; the metal ramrods flashed all at once in the sunshine as they were drawn from the barrels, turned in the air, and thrust into their sockets. The two sentinels fired again, independently and ineffectually.

The hunted man saw all this over his shoulder; he was now swimming vigorously with the current. His brain was as energetic as his arms and legs; he thought with the rapidity of lightning.

"The officer," he reasoned, "will not make that martinet's error a second time. It is as easy to dodge a volley as a single shot. He has probably already given the command to fire at will. God help me, I cannot dodge them all!"

An appalling plash within two yards of him was followed by a loud, rushing sound, *diminuendo,* which seemed to travel back through the air to the fort and died in an explosion which stirred the very river to its deeps! A rising sheet of water curved over him, fell down upon him, blinded him, strangled him! The cannon had taken a hand in the game. As he shook his head free from the commotion of the smitten water he heard the deflected shot humming through the air ahead, and in an instant it was cracking and smashing the branches in the forest beyond.

"They will not do that again," he thought; "the next time they will use a charge of grape. I must keep my eye upon the gun; the smoke will apprise me–the report arrives too late; it lags behind the missile. That is a good gun."

Suddenly he felt himself whirled round and round–spinning like a top. The water, the banks, the forests, the now distant bridge, fort and men–all were commingled and blurred. Objects were represented by their colors only; circular horizontal streaks of color—that was all he saw. He had been caught in a vortex and was being whirled on with a velocity of advance and gyration that made him giddy and sick. In a few moments he was flung upon the gravel at the foot of the left bank of the stream—the southern bank—and behind a projecting point which concealed him from his enemies. The sudden arrest of his motion, the abrasion of one of his hands on the gravel, restored him, and he wept with delight. He dug his fingers into the sand, threw it over himself in handfuls and audibly blessed it. It looked like diamonds, rubies, emeralds; he could think of nothing beautiful which it did not resemble. The trees upon the bank were giant garden plants; he noted a definite order in their arrangement, inhaled the fragrance of their blooms. A strange, roseate light shone through the spaces among their trunks and the wind made in their branches the music of aeolian harps. He had no wish to perfect his escape—was content to remain in that enchanting spot until retaken.

A whiz and rattle of grapeshot among the branches high above his head roused him from his dream. The baffled cannoneer had fired him a random farewell. He sprang to his feet, rushed up the sloping bank, and plunged into the forest.

All that day he traveled, laying his course by the rounding sun.

The forest seemed interminable; nowhere did he discover a break in it, not even a woodman's road. He had not known that he lived in so wild a region. There was something uncanny in the revelation.

By nightfall he was fatigued, footsore, famishing. The thought of his wife and children urged him on. At last he found a road which led him in what he knew to be the right direction. It was as wide and straight as a city street, yet it seemed untraveled. No fields bordered it, no dwelling anywhere. Not so much as the barking of a dog suggested human habitation. The black bodies of the trees formed a straight wall on both sides, terminating on the horizon in a point, like a diagram in a lesson in perspective. Overhead, as he looked up through this rift in the wood, shone great golden stars looking unfamiliar and grouped in strange constellations. He was sure they were arranged in some order which had a secret and malign significance. The wood on either side was full of singular noises, among which—once, twice, and again—he distinctly heard whispers in an unknown tongue.

His neck was in pain and lifting his hand to it found it horribly swollen. He knew that it had a circle of black where the rope had bruised it. His eyes felt congested; he could no longer close them. His tongue was swollen with thirst; he relieved its fever by thrusting it forward from between his teeth into the cold air. How softly the turf had carpeted the untraveled avenue—he could no longer feel the roadway beneath his feet!

Doubtless, despite his suffering, he had fallen asleep while walking, for now he sees another scene—perhaps he has merely recovered from a delirium. He stands at the gate of his own home. All is as he left it, and all bright and beautiful in the morning sunshine. He must have traveled the entire night. As he pushes open the gate and passes up the wide white walk, he sees a flutter of female garments; his wife, looking fresh and cool and sweet, steps down from the veranda to meet him. At the bottom of the steps she stands waiting, with a smile of ineffable joy, an attitude of matchless grace and dignity. Ah, how beautiful she is! He springs forward with extended arms. As he is about to clasp her he feels a stunning blow upon the back of the neck; a blinding white light blazes all about him with a sound like the shock of a cannon—then all is darkness and silence!

Peyton Farquhar was dead; his body, with a broken neck, swung gently from side to side beneath the timbers of the Owl Creek bridge.

A CLOSER LOOK

"Peyton Farquhar was dead; his body, with a broken neck, swung gently from side to side beneath the timbers of the Owl Creek bridge" (21). The last sentence of Ambrose Bierce's short story "An Occurrence at Owl Creek Bridge" is one of the most famous in all of American literature. But why does it carry so much import? It is a simple statement of fact; there is nothing earth-shattering about the words. But to a reader who has been wrapped up in the delusion of the condemned man, the words come as a shock, seemingly out of nowhere. To a careful reader, though, the ending should come as no surprise, for the author has made it clear what will happen from the very beginning.

The man on the bridge about to be hanged is a farmer named Peyton Farquhar, and from the looks of the company assembled, he has absolutely no chance of escaping. Apart from the sergeant, two soldiers, the captain, and the two sentinels who are all standing on the bridge, there are also "spectators," armed infantrymen from the fort nearby, who are watching the scene from the opposite bank. The only possible occurrence that day could be a hanging. The "doomed man" has desperate thoughts of escape that foreshadow the imagined events of the story's third part, but the facts are insurmountable: his hands are tightly bound, there is a noose about his neck, and the only thing separating him from death is the presence of another man on the opposite end of the board upon which they stand.

Time slows as Peyton nears execution. The "swirling water of the stream racing madly beneath his feet" becomes "sluggish" (9), and the ticking of his watch becomes an agonizingly accurate death knell, like a bell that is rung in a church to signal a funeral. He imagines his watch's "sharp, distinct, metallic percussion" piercing through his body like a knife, and we know that death is at hand. But what happens next is where readers can be led astray if we miss the signs that Bierce has planted.

As the sergeant steps off the plank, we are taken to a flashback of how Peyton came to be in this situation. Removed from the essential event of the story, we begin to lose focus, and, like Peyton, think of other possibilities that we know are impossible. For in the second section, we learn more of Peyton's character and should realize that this man, who is "ardently devoted to the Southern cause" and longs for "the larger life of the soldier, the opportunity for distinction" is deluding himself with visions of grandeur (10). He does not realize that he has been duped into a futile mission by a Federal scout—a Northern soldier pretending to be in the Southern army by his wearing of gray. We should, by now, be doubting Peyton's perspective.

When Peyton is hanged at the beginning of section three, he is plainly "as one already dead," and the story should come to an end (12). Yet Bierce again plays with time and shows us what might happen in the split-second that exists between living and dying. Because Peyton is being hanged over open water, it seems natural for him to equate hanging with drowning, and he feels as though he is descending into the stream when it is the noose around his neck that is providing "a sharp pressure upon his throat, followed by a sense of suffocation" (12). The sensation of sinking is perhaps more attributable to his inability to breathe, the feeling of "congestion" caused by a lack of oxygen to his brain.

In short, Bierce gives Peyton a near-death experience. Peyton is not escaping anywhere physically; he is transitioning between life and death. "Encompassed in a luminous cloud, of which he was now merely the fiery heart, without material substance" (13), Peyton is no longer alive, but he is not quite dead, either. He sees the proverbial light at the end of the tunnel, which is at first faint and seemingly far away but then grows brighter, and although he equates the bright light with the sun at the surface of the stream, it is actually death's door. When Peyton's "eyes were blinded by the sunlight; his chest expanded convulsively, and with a supreme and crowning agony his lungs engulfed a great draught of air," he is drawing his last breath, despite what he thinks is a return to life and a "full possession of his physical senses" (15). These senses are not real; they are imagined, for they are "preternaturally keen . . . they made record of things never before perceived" (15). But in Peyton Farquhar's final moment of life, his supernatural senses cannot save him, not even from his imagined escape through gunfire. For he has reached the farther shore of the afterlife, the sand that glimmers like diamonds, and despite his mad dash through uncharted territory, he has arrived at a new home from which he will never part.

ABOUT THE AUTHOR

Ambrose Bierce was born on July 24, 1842, on a farm in Ohio. Although he had seven siblings, his family was not close-knit, and his parents were religious to an extreme. He had a strong bond with an uncle, Lucius Bierce, who was more of a parent to the young Ambrose and who funded the teenager's early military training in the days preceding the American Civil War. At the age of 15, Bierce attended the Kentucky

The Battle of Shiloh

Military Institute for a single term before developing what would become a lifelong interest in journalism by serving as a printer's apprentice at a newspaper in the small town of Warsaw, Indiana.

In 1861, the 18-year-old Bierce volunteered to serve in the Union army, enlisting in the 9th Indiana Regiment (or Volunteers) for three months, as it was thought at the time that the war would be swift and conclude in a decisive victory for the North. After three months, though, with no end in sight, Bierce reenlisted and engaged in three years of continuous military action, fighting in such battles as Shiloh, Chickamauga,

Murfreesboro, and Chattanooga. On June 23, 1864, Bierce was seriously wounded at the Battle of Kennesaw Mountain by a bullet that glanced the side of his head. He may have experienced what we now call a near-death experience and used that later as inspiration for his famous short story "An Occurrence at Owl Creek Bridge." Bierce was sent home to recover but soon returned to active duty, marching in General William Tecumseh Sherman's army in Georgia during the last part of 1864 and remaining with the Union forces until the Confederacy's surrender in April 1865.

Bierce made his way west after the war as part of a surveying party, and by the end of 1866, he had reached San Francisco, California, where he took a job at the Federal Mint and spent the next two years honing his writing skills in private. In 1868, he landed a position with a weekly financial publication called the *San Francisco News Letter and Commercial Advertiser*, taking over a popular humor column and branding it with his own style of cutting satire and wit. From then until 1872, Bierce made a name for himself as *the* literary guru of the West Coast. In 1872, he and his new wife, Molly Day (whose family was prominent in San Francisco society), moved to London for three years, where Bierce's career continued to blossom and his first three books were published.

Upon the Bierces' return to the United States, the author spent short stints at editing several publications and even tried his hand at mining in the Dakota Territory. In 1887, he began writing for wealthy newspaper publisher William Randolph Hearst's *San Francisco Examiner*, where he would make his most enduring mark on journalism. Bierce also continued writing short stories, the majority of which were composed between 1882 and 1896. Bierce was unlike many authors in that he did not begin his career by writing in this form; his tales were written in his maturity and showed a polish and artistry reflective of his experience. He used incidents and inspiration from his own life as the basis for his short stories and preferred to write in three main genres: satirical horror, antiwar satires, and Western tall tales. The war stories, informed by the many terrifying events Bierce witnessed during the Civil War, were especially popular and powerful. His biting humor and criticism of everything from politics to the very essence of human nature—reflected in his nickname, "Bitter Bierce"—are usually at play in his work.

Like much of his writing, Bierce's life did not have a particularly happy ending. The writer, perhaps too dedicated to his craft, often distanced himself from his family, and as a result, he and his wife eventually separated, divorcing in 1904. His two sons died before him, one in a gunfight over a woman and the other from pneumonia. His daughter,

Ambrose Bierce

Mexican revolutionary leader Pancho Villa

Helen, was the only member of the family to survive far into the 20th century. Bierce's family troubles were often fodder for other members of the press, who used his failings as a father and husband to defame his character. But nothing or no one could curtail his writing. In 1906, one of Bierce's best-known works was published under the original title *The Cynic's Word Book*; later renamed *The Devil's Dictionary*, it was a collection of words and their ironic and satirical definitions. Between his *Dictionary*, journalism, and short stories, Bierce published an estimated four million words during his lifetime.

In 1913, Bierce embarked on a tour of Civil War battlefields and then made his way into Mexico, joining up (in an observatory role) with the revolutionary Pancho Villa, who was waging a rebellion against the Mexican government. The 71-year-old Bierce then disappeared–some believe he was killed during one of Villa's battles in 1914–never to be seen again. For a man who had written so many stories about war and critiqued the politics of his times, there could have been no more fitting path to take into the ultimate realm of the unknown.

Published by Creative Education

P.O. Box 227, Mankato, Minnesota 56002

Creative Education is an imprint of The Creative Company.

www.thecreativecompany.us

Design by Rita Marshall; production by Christine Vanderbeek

Page 22–31 text by Kate Riggs

Printed by Corporate Graphics in the United States of America

Photographs by Corbis (Bettmann, Medford Historical Society Collection),

Getty Images (Mansell/Time & Life Pictures)

Library of Congress Cataloging-in-Publication Data

Bierce, Ambrose, 1842–1914?

An occurrence at Owl Creek Bridge / by Ambrose Bierce.

p. cm. – (Creative short stories)

Summary: During the United States Civil War, a condemned man has many thoughts as he stands on a bridge, awaiting hanging. Includes an analysis of the story and a biography of the author.

ISBN 978-1-58341-922-9

1. Prisoners–Fiction. 2. United States–History–Civil War, 1861–1865–Fiction. I. Title. II. Series.

PZ7.B4766Oc 2010 [Fic]–dc22 2009027893 CPSIA: 120109 PO1090

First edition

2 4 6 8 9 7 5 3 1